This Little Tiger book belongs to:

_____

_____

_____

For Jason ~ N C

LITTLE TIGER PRESS
1 The Coda Centre, 189 Munster Road, London SW6 6AW
www.littletiger.co.uk

First published in Great Britain 2010
This edition published 2016

A CIP catalogue record for this book is available from the British Library

ISBN 978-1-84869-603-7

Printed in China • LTP/1800/1727/1016

2 4 6 8 10 9 7 5 3 1

Natalie Chivers

Rhino's Great BIG Itch!

LITTLE TIGER PRESS
London

Rhino had an itch – a great
big terrible itch,
right in his ear.

He twisted . . .

he turned . . .

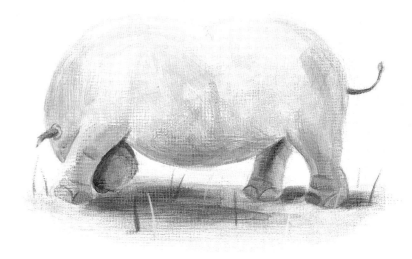

he wriggled,
he rolled . . .

But the itch just
wouldn't go.

"All you need is a little help!" said Bird.

"You're right!" said Rhino. So . . .

. . . off he went to find someone
to scratch his itch.

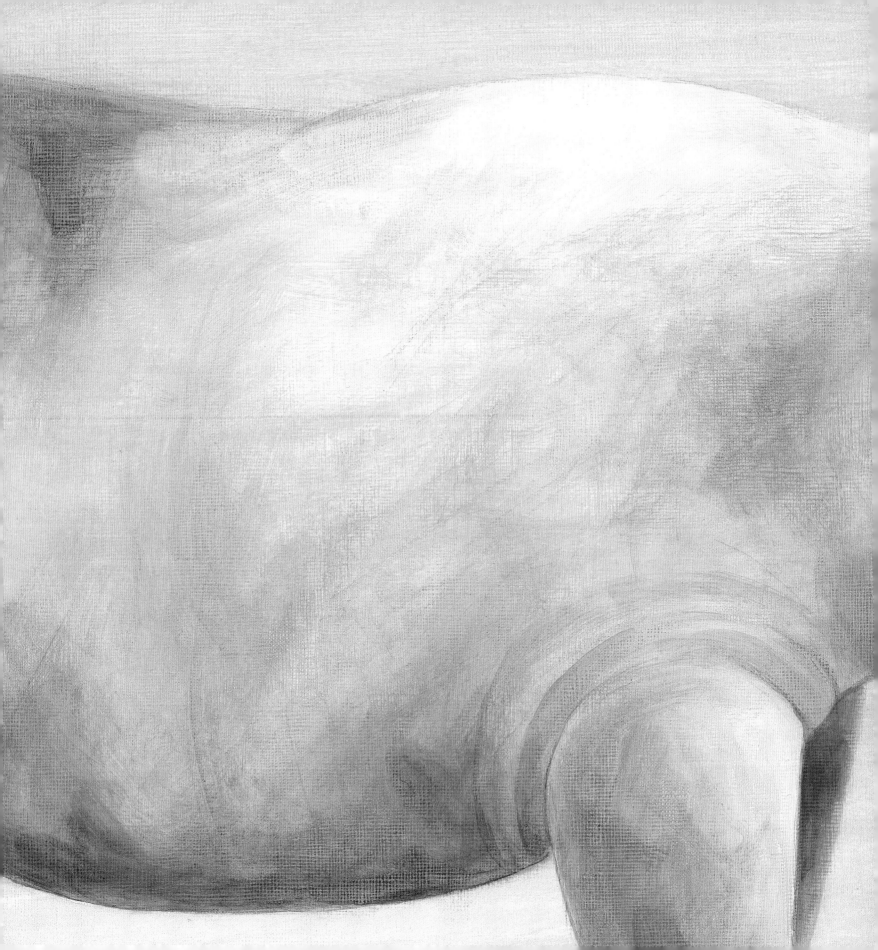

"Can **you** scratch my itch, Frog?"
Rhino asked.

But Frog was
too slimy.

Monkey was too silly.

Lizard was too
prickly.

And Rhino didn't even bother
to ask Lion!

It was no good.
The itch was still there.

"All I need is a little help!"
Rhino sighed.

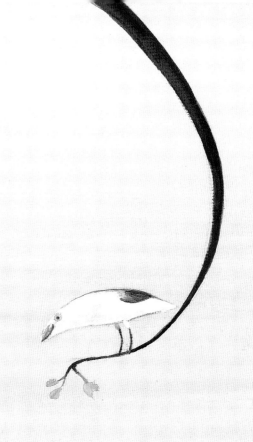

"I can help!"
said a little voice.

"How can **you** help, Bird?" asked Rhino.
"My itch is **big,** and you are far too tiny."

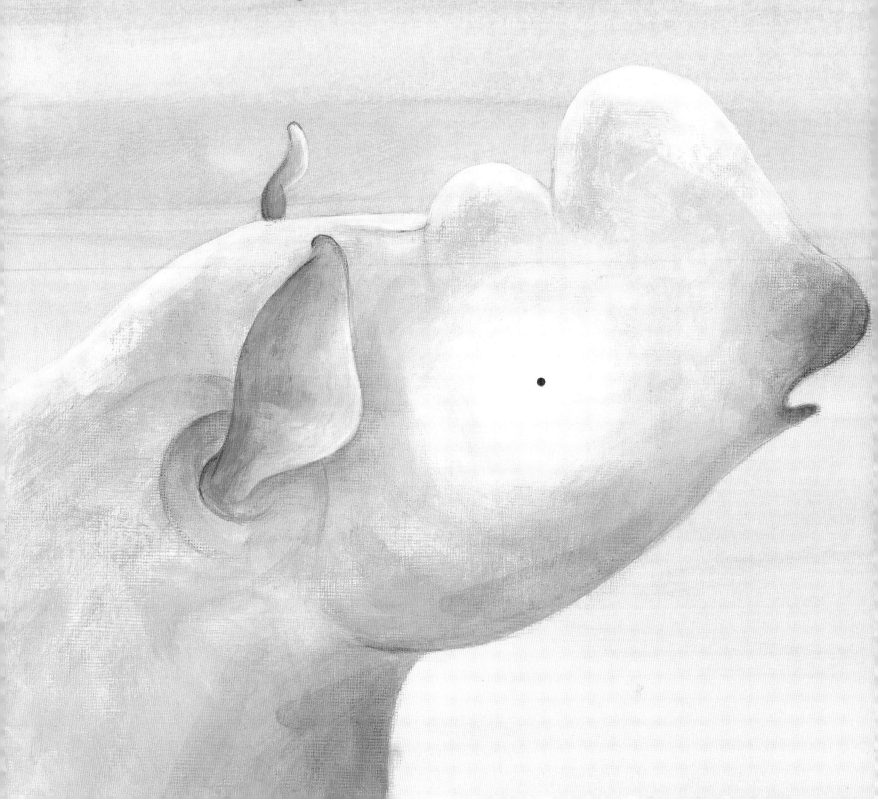

"I may be small," said Bird,
"but I am **just right** for you!"

So with
a hop . . .

and a skip . . .

and a little peck . . .

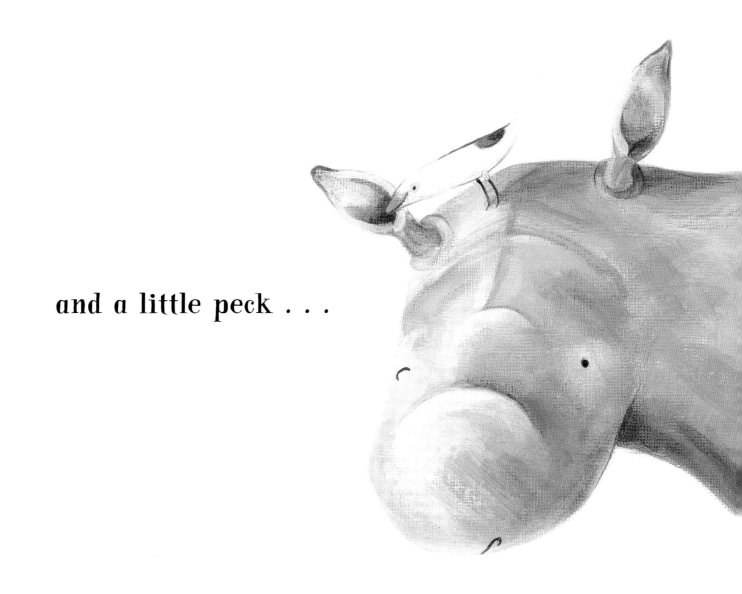

. . . the itch was gone!

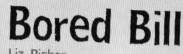
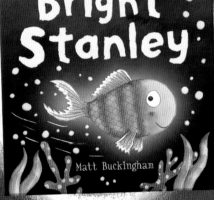

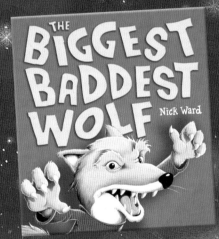